GW00870234

Murder at Teatime

Penelope Sotheby

Copyright © 2019 Penelope Sotheby

First published in 2019 by Jonmac Limited.

All rights reserved.

This book is a work of fiction. All names, characters and places, incidents are used entirely fictitiously. Any resemblance to actual events, or persons, living or dead, is entirely coincidental.

No part of this publication may be reproduced, or transmitted in any form or by any means, electronic or otherwise, without written permission from the publisher.

Free Book

Sign up for this author's new release mailing list and receive a free copy of her very first novella _Murder At The Inn_. This fantastic whodunit will keep you guessing to the very end and is not currently available anywhere else.

Go to http://fantasticfiction.info/murder-at-the-inn/ to have a look.

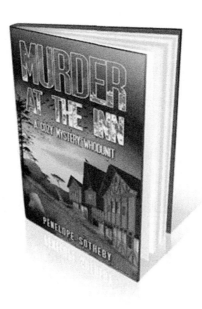

Other Books By The Author

Table of Contents

Chapter 1

Diane breathed in the sweet scent of the salt air through the open car window as Albert parked at the marina in Poole. It had been far too long since her last holiday and she felt her body relax as she climbed out of the car. The sound of music from the nearby quay made her smile as brightly colored flags fluttered in the breeze from the roofs of pubs and shops. During the summer Poole was crowded with tourists, but Diane didn't mind. Crowds and music were a part of summer at the shore, a summer she hoped was going to be uneventful.

Both Diane and Albert had some heartbreak recently as their dog Rufus, had passed on. This holiday was therefore something they planned to get away for a bit and to take their mind off of things. Albert would console Diane that Rufus had lived a long, and mostly good life, which Diane could not disagree with.

Reaching into the back seat for her laptop case and overnight bag, she was met with resistance by her husband, "Diane, you have been through a lot of stress lately. Let me worry about the bags, you just relax."

"Albert, I can't let you carry all of the bags, let me carry my laptop at least."

"If you insist, but I don't want you to worry about anything while we are at the boat, just have a good time."

"I'm with you, of course I'm going to have a good time," she said as she smiled at her adoring husband.

Albert Moreland was surprisingly strong for a retired solicitor. He shouldered the bags with the ease of a man half his age as they approached his sailboat. The wind whipped through Diane's hair and sung in the rigging of sailboats as they walked down the dock.

"There she is," said Albert as they approached Siren's Call, the forty-foot sailboat that Albert Moreland loved dearly. Diane detected a change in her husband's disposition as he stepped aboard the boat; he seemed younger and happier, like a kid with his favorite toy.

"Albert, she is beautiful. I thought you told me you were just going to do routine maintenance this year, but it looks like you have painted the deck," said Diane as she stepped aboard.

"Looks good, doesn't it? Clancy does a terrific job, he's worth every pound he charges," said Albert as he admired the work done to his boat.

Diane carried her laptop down below to the salon and set up her temporary workstation in the forward berth. A wood desk and navigation station made for an ideal office while she was aboard, Diane thought as she plugged in the power cord.

"I didn't bring you to Poole to spend all your time working, Mrs. Moreland," teased Albert.

"Sorry dear, but it's still Dimbleby," Diane smirked. "I know you didn't, but you never can tell, I may be inspired while we are on the water. I promise I will only write when you have gone to sleep. I want to spend every minute with you," she assured her husband as she joined him in the salon.

"No murders, no police detectives, those are the rules of this holiday," he replied.

"I promise, no murders on this trip, I won't even go fishing," she answered as her husband embraced her.

"Diane. Let's just have fun, go sailing and enjoy being together. The rest of the world can disappear for a few days, it will be there waiting for us when we get home."

"Albert, you are right, it's just you, me and Siren's Call for the next few days. I can't think of better company."

The following morning, Diane and Albert untied the lines and pointed Siren's Call to deep waters. The sun was shining overhead and sparkled on the waves as the sailboat motored out of the marina. It was a perfect morning and Diane could not imagine being happier than she was at that moment.

Albert steered the boat out of the channel as Diane raised the mainsail and then the foresail. The wind filled the sails, carrying Siren's Call away from the shore. Diane looked at the houses along the water's edge as they grew smaller in her view. All her cares and stress were left on land as the sleek fiberglass boat heeled over gently and cut through the waves.

For five days, Diane enjoyed the holiday she had dreamed of. The weather was warm, with only a small squall late in the afternoon on the first day. Being aboard the boat she settled into the lackadaisical routine of a boating holiday. Meals were prepared in the galley without rushing, dinner every evening was an event and there was always time for drinks at sunset after anchoring.

She described the holiday as a second honeymoon and Albert agreed; the romance of life aboard the boat was inescapable. Diane was not sure she wanted to return home. Living in Albert's house was lovely, and the garden bloomed with fragrant flowers this time of year. The library always welcomed her for an hour's reading, but in Apple Mews, she was a mystery novelist and an amateur sleuth. She enjoyed both aspects of her life immensely but they could be stressful, especially when she knew the victims as she often did. Being on the boat with Albert had a way of simplifying her life; there were no clues to follow, no suspects to interview.

Diane enjoyed the rest as she pondered what she would be if she didn't solve mysteries. Laying on the deck of the boat, she came up with an answer - she didn't know what activity she would pursue because solving mysteries was in her blood. At her age, many ladies were devoted to gardening, to crochet and needlework, even volunteer work. Diane knew in her heart that as much as she enjoyed the rest, assisting Inspector Crothers was her way of feeling useful.

But like all good things, the holiday came to an end. Diane and Albert eventually had to return home, as Albert was due to give a speech at the retirement dinner of a colleague on Friday. Diane prepared a meal worthy of a gourmet chef on the last night on the boat as they settled in for a sunset that promised to be spectacular. Raising their wine glasses to each other, the boat and their holiday, Diane made Albert promise that he would take her out on Siren's Call more often. Albert wholeheartedly agreed as they drank the white wine and watched the sun slide behind the clouds on the horizon.

After a week on the water, Diane felt relaxed even as Albert negotiated the traffic on their drive back home. The radio in the car was set to a classical music station and light rain fell on the windshield. Diane remarked that the weather had held out beautifully for their holiday. Listening to the weather report on the radio, the rain was supposed to set in for the weekend. The rain promised many hours spent with a cup of tea and a good book, thought Diane as Albert exited the busy highway, heading for the bucolic village of Apple Mews.

Chapter 2

Albert and Diane arrived home just before dinner. They were met at the door by Deidre, who promised that a hot meal would be on the table by the time they freshened up. Diane rifled through the pile of unopened mail in the study as Albert checked the voicemail. Deidre announced that dinner was served as she gave Diane a message she had taken earlier in the week.

Diane's eyes scanned the message written in Deidre's slightly untidy script, "Deidre, did you write that Inspector Crothers needs to speak to me or Albert?" asked Diane.

Deidre looked at the message and shook her head, "Honestly ma'am, I can't remember exactly, but I do remember that he tried to leave a voicemail message. He told me it was full, I think he wants you to call him."

"I wonder why he didn't call me on my mobile phone?" asked Diane

"We were out of range, remember? We left the world behind," said Albert as he kissed Diane's cheek.

"That's right. Deidre, did he say if it was urgent?"

Deidre answered with a shrug, "I don't remember, but if the Inspector called looking for you, I don't think he was calling to chat."

"You are probably right, I will give him a call," said Diane as she picked up the phone in the study. "Albert, I hope it's nothing serious," she said as she punched in the number.

"If he called us, I doubt it could be anything other than serious," Albert replied.

"Inspector Crothers," answered a familiar voice.

"Inspector, Diane here, I just arrived home."

"Am I glad to hear your voice, I have something that I need to discuss with you and Albert. When would be a good time to stop in?" he asked.

"Would after dinner this evening be too soon?" asked Diane.

"Not soon enough, what time? How does eight o'clock sound?"

"Eight o'clock will be fine, we will see you then," said Diane as she placed the phone back on the charger.

Albert glanced at his watch and said, "We haven't been home for half an hour."

"I know, do you think it's too late to get back in the car? My bags are still packed," Diane said with a sigh.

"Did he say what this was about, what happened while we were away?"

"He neglected to tell me, but he did say something rather interesting. He is coming not only to see me, but this time, he needs to see you too."

"See me, whatever for? I am not an amateur detective like you," Albert replied.

"I'm sure we will find out the answer to that question soon enough, as he'll be arriving at eight o'clock this evening."

"Well, in that case, we better enjoy the last few hours of our holiday. Whenever the police are involved I know you won't have a moment's rest until the case is solved."

Diane looked at Albert with a quizzical expression, "And what makes you think there is a case to be solved?"

"Inspector Crothers is coming to see you, to see us under mysterious circumstances. That can only mean one thing: someone is dead and there is a mystery that needs to be solved."

Diane could not argue with her husband's assessment of the situation. As he held the chair for her at the dining room table, she thought about the days they spent on Siren's Call and how far away the world was from the sailboat. As she reached for a dinner roll, she knew the world was just a text or phone call away when she was on shore. As Albert said, they had only a few more hours until they were once again part of the world of murder, intrigue, and danger that always accompanied Inspector Crothers when he came to call.

Diane tried to focus on the delicious meal that Deidre prepared for their first night home; roasted vegetables were the ideal complement to sole in parchment with lemon dressing. Diane complemented Deidre on the meal as she ordered a pot of tea and light sandwiches in preparation for Inspector Crothers' impending visit.

Diane waited in the drawing room for the Inspector and found herself unable to concentrate on the book in her hand. Ordinarily, any meeting with Inspector Crothers was not a source of anxiety for her, but then he didn't usually ask to speak to Albert. Staring at the page of the novel, her mind drifted to the hours of contentment on Siren's Call. As much as she hated to admit it, on shore she was needed in a way that she would never be on the boat.

She was aware that not many retired school teachers enjoyed a second career as detectives. Although Diane may not win awards for her prize roses or baking skills, she contributed peace of mind to the community of Apple Mews every time a dangerous murderer was arrested. The work was heartbreaking at times, especially when she was acquainted with the victims, but she knew that Inspector Crothers was grateful for every piece of advice that she gave him.

As she watched the raindrops strike the window of the drawing room, Deidre quietly sat down a pot of tea and sandwiches on the tea table. Glancing at her watch, Diane saw that it was nearly eight o'clock. Inspector Crothers would be arriving soon and she wondered what could be keeping Albert. As Deirdre left, Albert walked slowly into the room, his face in a frown.

"Albert, what's wrong?" Diane asked as she closed the book, placing the novel on the table beside the ornately upholstered chair.

"I was listening to the voicemail and returning calls. I'm afraid there had been a bit of bad news while we were away. Mrs. Tamarland has died."

"Mrs. Tamarland?" asked Diane, "Mrs. John Tamarland from church?"

"She was an old client of mine. A bit of a recluse in her later years if I remember correctly, but a pleasant woman."

"I don't recall her as being particularly involved with the church. She attended services on a regular basis but I can't remember the last time she stayed for tea," said Diane as the doorbell rang. "That must be the Inspector."

Deidre showed the Inspector into the drawing room. Diane watched as his eyes fell on the pot of tea and plate of sandwiches. "Inspector, it is good to see you, I had Deidre prepare a plate of sandwiches for you. I know you rarely eat properly when you are working."

"You know me well, a cup of tea and a bite to eat would be most welcome," he said as Diane poured tea into a cup.

"Inspector, Diane tells me that you needed to see both of us, what is this about?" asked Albert.

"I regret to inform you that a woman of your acquaintance has died, a Mrs. John Tamarland," answered the Inspector as he reached for a cold chicken sandwich.

"I was afraid that was the case, I only discovered her death moments before you arrived," Albert said.

"Then you are aware that this is a murder investigation," Inspector Crothers said as he bit into the sandwich.

"A murder investigation? No, I was not aware of that," Albert replied, a shocked look on his face. "Inspector, how did she die? I was under the impression it was from natural causes."

"I'm afraid not, she died as result of a gunshot wound delivered at close range. I am not surprised that you were not aware of that fact, as we've been trying to keep the details of her death out of the press as much as possible. All the papers have reported that her death was ruled as suspicious, but that is all the information I have permitted to be leaked."

"A gunshot wound? Was it a home invasion, a burglary perhaps?" asked Diane.

"It doesn't appear to be the case. From all indications, it would appear that Mrs. Tamarland knew her killer. There were no signs of forced entry into the residence or a struggle. A pot of tea and two cups sat on the tea table of her drawing room. The scene looked as sociable as this one except for the body of Mrs. Tamarland discovered only steps from the sofa."

"Were there any clues, any notes?" asked Diane.

"Not a single note or calling card for her mysterious guest. The victim was holding an empty plate in her hand when she was shot, we discovered its shattered remains on the floor beside her. We have reason to believe that whoever was responsible for her killing was a social acquaintance, friend or family member."

"And you are certain her guest was the murderer?" asked Albert.

"It would appear so, there were traces of gunpowder on the teacup handle. Whoever killed Mrs. Tamarland shot her to death, then finished his or her cup of tea after she died."

"How very odd, that someone would be so cold-blooded as to finish their tea after committing murder but not methodical enough to clean up the evidence. Tell me Inspector, have you been able to identify any fingerprints or DNA samples from the teacup?"

"We sent the teacup to London to a crime lab, but I have to confess that I am not optimistic about the conclusion. There have been no discernable fingerprints. It seems that the killer may have been wearing gloves. The DNA evidence from the teacup has not been identified, and there is concern that the rim of the cup was wiped clean with a cleaning solution."

"You don't think it's strange that the killer thought to remove DNA evidence from the rim of the cup but neglected the gunpowder residue, or bothered to clean the cup and put it in the cabinet? It seems that the killer is smart but absent-minded," said Diane, "or an amateur."

"I have to admit that nothing about this case is simple. Mrs. Tamarland lived in the country, she did not have nearby neighbors to see her visitor or hear the gunshot. She has a maid but the woman comes once a week and was not working that day. It was the maid that discovered the body the following morning when she reported to work."

"Was anything missing, taken from the house, anything of value?" asked Diane.

"Nothing at all, Mrs. Tamarland's purse was on the table in the foyer, her jewelry box on her dresser upstairs in her bedroom. It appears that the person was at her residence for one reason and one reason only, to kill her."

"Inspector, what can I do to help?" asked Albert.

"Mr. Moreland, as Mrs. Tamarland was a widow with almost no family or friends, I was hoping you might be able to provide some information. I am aware that you represented her over the years, your card was found in a prominent position in her wallet."

"What kind of information did you require?" Albert asked.

"Are you aware of any business dealings, any changes to her will, or any other information that may prove useful to this investigation?"

"Not that I am aware of. I completed a will for her many years ago. I cannot recall any other information that would be relevant."

"Even information that would seem irrelevant would be helpful at this stage in the investigation," admitted the Inspector as he reached for a second chicken sandwich.

"I have been retired for several years but if I can recall anything that may be useful to your investigation I will be sure to pass it along."

"Thank you Mr. Moreland, I am grateful for your help," said the Inspector.

"Inspector, what about the will? Who stood to gain from Mrs. Tamarland's death?" asked Diane.

"A nephew, a Mr. Thomas Tamarland lately of York."

"Lately of York?" asked Diane.

"I say lately because he has been incarcerated for several years."

"Incarcerated? That seems like a good place to start," said Diane.

"Perhaps, but he has been charged with petty thievery, money laundering and scams targeting pensioners. He seems to be content to be a garden variety low life."

"You mean that he does not have a history of violent crime, not even a bar brawl or a fight?" asked Albert.

"Not one incident of violence, so for him to step up to killing his aunt would be a drastic escalation."

"But it is possible, isn't it?" asked Diane as she poured a second cup of tea, her interest piqued.

"Possible but unlikely. As far as I have been able to ascertain, he didn't even realize he was her sole heir until after her death. The only people that knew of her will were Mrs. Tamarland and your office, Mr. Moreland. For a petty criminal like her nephew, her wallet, television, and jewelry would have proven to be tempting targets," said the Inspector.

"Unless he's smarter than you think, he may have known about the will. She may have told him and he's lying," said Diane.

"Maybe so, but he just doesn't strike me as being that smart or that cold-blooded, which leaves me with no other suspect," the Inspector said as he sighed.

"Sounds like you need some help," said Diane.

"Thank you, you know I could always use your help," he said as he appeared to perk up, "May I have a bit more tea?" asked the Inspector as Diane poured tea into his empty cup and realized that her holiday was over. She was home.

Chapter 3

It was two in the morning and Diane found it impossible to sleep. The rain thundered onto the stone pavers outside the kitchen window as she waited for the water to boil in the kettle. The death of Mrs. Tamarland was unexpected and Diane could not stop thinking about the circumstances of the woman's murder. Diane had seen people come to violent ends before this case, but there was something about this murder that was very unsettling.

The kettle whistled, startling Diane. Reaching for the kettle, she turned the burner off and poured the water in her cup. Cold shivers ran along her spine as she thought about the killer finishing his or her cup of tea as Mrs. Tamarland was taking her last breath. There was something about that scenario that felt disturbing. The murderer knew Mrs. Tamarland and was in no hurry to leave the scene. Diane agreed with the Inspector; this was not a random act of violence, this was personal.

Diane sat down at the kitchen table and held the steaming cup in her hands. There was a detail about the murder that she was certain that the Inspector and she were overlooking. A murderer that stayed for tea did not seem to be overly concerned about getting caught? Was it overconfidence, or some other reason? Perhaps, thought Diane, it was that grimly casual attitude that may provide a clue or a lead.

In her experience, people that committed murders typically tried to get away with the crime. This person did too, but only to a point; wearing gloves and wiping the teacup rim were indicators that the killer did not want to be discovered, but the murderer did not flee immediately after firing the gun. Did the killer want to gloat over Mrs. Tamarland or be sure she was dead? It was a grisly affair, to imagine a member of the church coming to such a cold, terrible end.

Diane did not know much about Mrs. Tamarland's earlier years, but the woman that she knew hardly seemed the type that would arouse a deep hatred in other people. She kept to herself, was not unkind or rude and when she did speak, she seemed to be a pleasant person. Diane did not recall ever thinking that Mrs. Tamarland was anything other than what she seemed - a quiet, reclusive widow.

Although Diane was not a close acquaintance of the victim, she recalled Mrs. Tamarland as being generous when it came to supporting charities and church benefits. In all her years in the congregation, Diane did not remember a single person saying one bad word about the murdered woman. The knowledge that the deceased was well regarded, quiet and possessed a generous nature made her manner of death even more perplexing.

The hands on the clock on the wall slowly moved and the rain continued to beat against the windows as Diane sat at the table, lost in thought. Her cup of tea turned cold before she remembered it. She detested cold tea but was not raised to be wasteful. Drinking the beverage, she glanced at the clock; it was still far too early, or too late depending on perspective, to rouse Inspector Crothers from his sleep.

Diane wanted to view the crime scene for herself, a method she found helped tremendously when she didn't have any other leads to follow. For two hours, Diane sat in the kitchen, her mind turning like gears as she tried to make sense of Mrs. Tamarland's murder. There was no doubt about it, she needed to visit the woman's house. Only then would Diane be certain that she would be able to offer sound advice to Inspector Crothers.

After the clock struck four in the morning, Diane left the kitchen and made her way quietly up the stairs. She was tired from her sleepless night and decided that she would attempt to get a few hours of rest. Crawling into bed, she was surprised to find Albert awake.

"Darling, are you still up?" he said.

"Yes, I couldn't sleep. I hope I didn't wake you."

"No, you didn't, I have been lying here, listening to the rain."

"I made a cup of tea, but that was two hours ago," Diane said as she lay back on the pillows.

"Mrs. Tamarland? Is that why you can't sleep?" he asked as he rolled over on his side.

"Yes, Albert it is. I can't make sense of it, can you? She was your client; can you think of any reason why someone would kill her and then have tea?"

Albert frowned, "I honestly can't. The firm represented many clients and she was one that I don't recall ever giving anyone at the office a moment's trouble. She seemed rather ordinary and quiet if you ask me."

"That is my dilemma. I am having difficulty imagining that she ever upset anyone to the point of cold-blooded murder."

"She must have upset someone to end up murdered," Albert concluded.

"I agree, but it doesn't make sense. Did she lead a double life? Who would want to kill a sweet, quiet widow and not take anything?" said Diane, "If this was random, I could understand, but it clearly wasn't and that is what I find to be so frustrating."

"Diane, don't let it frustrate you, try to get some sleep," Albert said as he kissed her cheek.

Diane turned off the lamp on the bedside table and stared into the darkness. Closing her eyes, she drifted into a restless sleep until morning. The alarm rang only a few hours later, Diane reached over to turn it off as Albert wished her good morning. She was exhausted and wanted to sleep until lunch, but she had an important call to make after breakfast.

Slowly dragging herself out of bed, Diane showered and dressed for the day. Staring at her reflection in the mirror, she could see dark circles under his eyes. She looked like she felt, tired. Resisting the urge to lay back down, she waited for Albert to finish dressing for breakfast.

"Would you like Deidre to bring a tray up so that you can rest?" Albert said as he looked at Diane, an expression of concern on his face.

"I look exhausted, I am sure of it, but I will be fine after a good breakfast. I hope Deirdre hasn't made anything healthy this morning, I need a plate filled with unhealthy fried foods and sausages."

"That sounds delicious, although I am not so sure your doctor would approve," teased Albert. "Shall we go down and find out what it shall be? Porridge with fresh fruit, egg white omelet or a decent breakfast?"

"Deidre tries to look after us, I would expect a boiled egg, slices of melon and a piece of dry toast if we are lucky."

Diane was not wrong about Deidre's motives, although she was slightly incorrect about the breakfast, as the yogurt with fresh fruit and toast were the main course. The tea was hot and strong and to Diane, that was far more important than a decadent fried breakfast with sausages and mushrooms.

After two cups of tea, and a generous portion of healthy yogurt, Diane felt as though she was prepared to face the daunting task that lay in front of her. As Albert read the morning paper, she called the Inspector. Leaving a message, she waited for him to return her call. She did not have long to wait, as he called less than five minutes later.

"Inspector, you must be busy this morning."

"I am, but never too busy for your call, so to what do I owe the pleasure?"

"I don't know if this is possible at this stage in the investigation, but I would like to view the crime scene for myself."

"You are in luck, forensics is finished with the preliminaries. I don't see why you can't view it if you choose. When did you have in mind?"

"That is entirely dependent upon your schedule."

"I have this afternoon free after three, do you have the address?"

"Mrs. Tamarland lived in Greenfield, is that correct? Which end, north or south?"

"North, you won't be able to miss her house. It is at the end of the lane, a large red brick place, used to be a parsonage."

"Oh yes, I know the one, how does half past three sound?"

"I will see you then," the Inspector replied.

Albert smiled at his wife and slipped his hand into hers. "You are going to the Tamarland residence, would you like for me to accompany you?"

"Only if you would like to go, I won't be long," Diane answered.

"Be home for dinner?" he asked with a smile.

"I wouldn't miss it," she said.

Chapter 4

After breakfast, Diane drove into town and attended her yoga class and stopped by the church. The doors were unlocked and the sanctuary was empty. It was quiet inside as she walked towards the pew that Mrs. Tamarland liked to occupy during services. Sitting where the late widow sat for so many Sundays, Diane tried to think about life from the woman's perspective. Did she have any enemies, anyone that would benefit from her death? As Diane sat in the pew, she could not recall any disharmony or discord in the woman's life. If it existed, it was like the woman herself, quiet and well hidden from the public.

Diane left the church and returned home, Albert was occupied by his speech that he was to deliver that Friday. Diane sat down at her laptop to write a few pages before her meeting with the Inspector. Finding it difficult to concentrate, Diane was relieved when she glanced at her watch and saw the time; she was due to meet the Inspector in half an hour. Kissing Albert goodbye, she walked outside to the car, troubled by her lack of concentration.

This was not like her, she thought as she turned the key in the ignition and shifted the car into reverse. Of all the cases she had ever worked on with Inspector

Crothers, she could not recall being consumed by facts but without a solid lead to follow. It had been less than twenty hours since she became aware of the mystery surrounding Mrs. Tamarland's death, but it felt like much longer for Diane. Hoping that the Inspector would have new information to share, she drove towards the widow's residence.

Diane pulled into the driveway behind the car that she easily recognized. The Inspector was already there when she arrived. Parking the car, she walked towards the house, carefully inspecting the residence. The brick two-story house appeared to be plain but well built. Two chimneys rose from opposite ends of the roof, a green vine climbed past a front window. A modest garden wall was shaded by trees and birds sang in the branches. It was a comfortable, peaceful place, rather like the woman that once called it home.

Ringing the bell, Diane patiently stood on the porch enjoying the view of the fields and pastures across the road when the door opened to reveal Inspector Crothers. Like Diane, he had dark circles around his eyes, and looked haggard and tired.

"Diane, please come in."

"Inspector, I don't mean to sound rude, but you didn't sleep very well last night, did you?"

"No, and neither did you," he smiled.

"It's this case, there are no solid leads and the way she died is disturbing," said Diane as she walked inside the house, "unless you have some other details you would like to share with me."

"Nothing new to tell. I'm afraid that we are forced to work with no witnesses, no neighbors' testimonies and very little evidence."

"Sounds like a challenge," Diane answered. "Is this the room where Mrs. Tamarland was killed?"

"It is, you will find it exactly as it was when she died. We have taken care not to disturb a single piece of furniture as this is still an ongoing investigation."

Diane slowly walked across the floor, her eyes scanning the room. The room, like the house, was modest but comfortable. A Chippendale sofa sat on a pastel Persian rug, a table set for afternoon tea sat in front of the sofa. The tea service was a simple white, blue and violet pattern that complemented the colors of the furnishings. The chairs matched the sofa in style and were a solid rose color with light blue accent pillows. A dark brown stain on the edge of the rug marked where Mrs. Tamarland had taken her final breath.

Walking from the room where Mrs. Tamarland was killed, Diane went to the kitchen and the study on the ground floor. There were no drawers open in the desk, no papers shuffled through in a hurry. The room looked as peaceful as it had the day the killer arrived for afternoon tea. Sighing, Diane walked upstairs and toured the bedrooms. Clothes hung in the closet in the master bedroom, the bed neatly made, throw pillows arranged symmetrically.

From her brief tour of the residence, she discovered that Mrs. Tamarland was organized, neat and was not a person that was prone to clutter. On the bedside table, a picture of the widow and her late husband taken many years ago, when they appeared to be in their twenties, was the only decoration. It was a touching detail and one that nearly brought a tear to her eye as she walked downstairs to join the Inspector.

"What do you think?" he asked as she walked into the drawing room.

"Everything seems to be in order, just as you described it to be. There is nothing out of place. If the killer was looking for something in this house, he or she was not in a rush."

"You are beginning to understand my dilemma, someone killed this woman in cold blood. Someone who may very well be living in our community. I have to find the killer and I have very little to go on."

"This may not be what you want to hear, but the nephew may be the best suspect you have. Just because we don't think he would kill his aunt doesn't mean he didn't do it."

"I had thought of that, Sergeant Webster and I are going to interview him this evening. He works at a repair shop and he gets off work after six."

"With his history, he may have owed money or became involved with something other than petty theft, he may have graduated to hardcore drug use. It's unlikely, but he is the only person that would have directly benefitted from her death."

"That we know of at this stage in the investigation. Even if he isn't a strong candidate for suspect, he may be able to tell us some details about his aunt's life. She was so secretive about her affairs that this case may be the most difficult of my career."

Diane was about to agree with his assessment when she thought of Mrs. Tamarland's reclusive lifestyle. Thinking about how tidy the house was, she thought about Deirdre. Deidre knew details of her life that few outside the house would ever be aware of. Deidre saw the mail, made tea for guests, overheard snippets of conversations.

"You may be forgetting a person that knows more about Mrs. Tamarland than her nephew or anyone else, her maid."

"Her maid worked one day a week," answered the Inspector.

"Yes, but she worked here every week and saw Mrs. Tamarland on a regular basis. She was the person that discovered the body."

"Diane, you may be onto something, I don't know why I didn't think of her. Sergeant Webster took a statement from her, but he didn't interview her."

"What do you know about her?" asked Diane.

"Not much, her name is Ruth Hedley, she is married, in her fifties."

"Ruth Hedley? That name doesn't ring a bell, is she from Apple Mews?"

"No, she lives half an hour away."

"Inspector, I don't think an interview with Mrs. Hedley would be a bad idea, she may be the break in the case you are looking for."

"I will ring her tomorrow. Thanks Diane, is there anything else you would suggest?"

As Diane looked around the room once more, she thought about what she did when she came home in the evening from an errand to town. She had a certain place that she sat her purse and Deidre would give her the mail or take her packages. Thinking of her routine, she had another question for the Inspector. "Mrs. Tamarland's will only mentioned the nephew, is that correct?"

"Yes, there does not seem to be any amendments or changes."

"What about her finances? Anything unusual in her spending or shopping habits? Any changes to her finances or unusual activity? Was there anything missing from her purse, any credit cards or cheques?"

"Her purse was examined and it still contained her wallet, all of her credit cards, her chequebook and ledger. There were nearly fifty pounds in cash in her purse."

"And her finances, any changes to her banking?"

"I have requested the statements for the last three months, I should have those by the end of the week, but I can call and demand that they send them to me immediately."

"Yes, I would start there and interview the maid. The killer drank tea after shooting the widow, confident that the crime would never be solved. That kind of confidence is either the result of careful planning or abject stupidity. Either way, there must be some small detail that will lead us to the murderer, we just have to look under every stone."

"Are we done here?" asked the Inspector.

"Yes, we are," said Diane as they walked out of Mrs. Tamarland's house together. Just as they were approaching their vehicles, Diane turned to the Inspector, "Forensics has done a sweep of the house, and their results?"

"Nothing conclusive so far."

"You said that Mrs. Tamarland was found by the sofa, that is where the blood stain was located on the rug. The killer would have been sitting in one of the chairs, the chairs with the accent pillows."

"I think I see what you are getting at," the Inspector answered. "I will have the forensics team do another sweep, this time concentrating on the furniture and the pillows in more detail."

"They may not turn up anything useful but without any leads to go on, I don't think being especially thorough will be a waste of time."

The Inspector agreed as they said their goodbyes. Diane slid into the driver's seat of her car and gazed at the house with the modest garden. Mrs. Tamarland spent her last years in the house and the last minutes of her life; it was peaceful and serene. It seemed like an injustice that Mrs. Tamarland would have to die violently in a place that was so tranquil. As she turned onto the lane, she vowed that she would help find Mrs. Tamarland's killer, a person so cold that Diane feared for the consequences for Apple Mews if they failed.

Chapter 5

The rain fell in a mist making the air outside the vehicle muggy, a change of pace for the weather in Shropshire. Inspector Crothers was grateful for the air conditioner in the car as he and Sergeant Webster sat in the parked car. They waited patiently in front of a row of townhouses that had been converted into flats, waiting for Mrs. Tamarland's nephew to return home after work.

"I bet he's at the pub," Sergeant Webster said as he peered out the windscreen.

Inspector Crothers nodded his head, "You're probably right. With his history, he doesn't seem like the sort that would come right home after work, whip up a gourmet dinner and spend a quiet evening at home."

"We will be lucky if he makes it home by midnight. Looks like we are in for a long night. Seems like old times, doesn't it Inspector? Reminds me of a stakeout."

"You mean the endless hours sitting in a car, trading life stories and praying you don't have to use the loo?"

"Sounds like you know the drill," the Sergeant replied. "All we need is a cup of tea, a few biscuits and something from the chippy and we are in business."

"If he isn't home by eight, we will see him at work tomorrow. I should have done that already," the Inspector said with a frown.

"You were just giving him the benefit of the doubt. It's hard enough to keep a good job with his kind of record. A detective nosing around asking him questions at work wouldn't look good."

"It's just my kind-hearted nature," the Inspector answered, "Although, after reading his history about swindling retirees out of their money, I'm not sure how inclined I really am to be kind to him."

"These people work their whole lives, and he waltzes in and takes them for what he can. I hope five years in prison made him see the error of his ways."

"As sole heir to his aunt's estate, he may be doing more than swindling these days."

"Looks like we are about to have a chance to find out, there's a man coming up the street that might be our guy."

"Sergeant, if that is Thomas Tamarland, we aren't going to get a chance to clog our arteries with fried food anytime, maybe after the interview."

Inspector Crothers waited for the figure to come closer to the car. The man was in his early thirties, thin to the point of being lanky and sporting shoulder-length hair. Working at an auto repair shop, his uniform should have been stained and dirty, but it was clean and slightly wrinkled. As the Inspector turned off the car, he had already made an observation about Thomas Tamarland; he was either a cautious mechanic who managed to keep his uniform clean, or he did very little work.

Inspector Crothers and Sergeant Webster approached the man as he was opening the door of the bottom flat of a townhouse. He did not seem to be surprised to see two officers suddenly appear at his house, a sign that he had experience being the subject of inquiry and interrogation.

"Well, well, what brings you two fine gentlemen to my humble abode?" he said with a smirk.

"Thomas Tamarland, I am Inspector Crothers, this is Sergeant Webster, we would like to ask you a few questions."

"You police types always do, I haven't got anything to hide so come in. I had to fire the maid, hard to get good help these days, don't mind the mess," Thomas said as he pushed the door to the flat open.

The flat was tiny, just a studio and a bathroom. The smell of cigarette smoke, mildew, and stale beer was overwhelming, but Thomas didn't seem to notice as he slid a pile of clothes and papers off the card table, "There we go, somewhere for you gentlemen to sit, hope you are going to be okay with the folding chairs, they are cheap but get the job done."

Inspector Crothers was reluctant to sit down in the flat. His eyes watered from the mildew growing on every surface and he was convinced that he would have to throw away the suit he was wearing after leaving the residence. As he sat down on the rickety folding chair, he thought of the flats he had visited over the years, and this one he decided was among the worst.

Thomas Tamarland walked across the dingy, gray carpet and opened a mini fridge, selecting a can of beer, "Since you two are my guests, I have to ask, either one of you want one?"

"Thank you, no, we are still on duty," the Inspector answered as he decided to charge ahead with the questions. Glancing at the Sergeant, he could tell from Sergeant Webster's facial expression that they both wanted to get out of there as soon as possible.

"That's better for me, it means I don't have to share," Thomas replied, laughing, as he took a seat on the bed. "You didn't come here for a social call, what can I do for you? There's a match on at 7.45 I have an interest in, not trying to be rude, but let's get to it."

Inspector Crothers answered, "I couldn't agree more, let's get to it. You are aware that you are your Aunt's sole heir to the estate, all of her property and any holdings or investments she may have had will go to you, is that correct?"

The man seated on the bed smiled from ear to ear as he raised his can of beer and said, "Here's to the old girl, you bet I know about it. I can't wait to tell that man I work for what he can do with this job as soon as the lawyer gets the paperwork settled."

"Were you close to your aunt? She must have thought a lot of you to leave you everything she owned?" asked Sergeant Webster.

Thomas gulped the beer and replied, "Close? I'm not going to lie, I wouldn't say we were close. In my younger days, she would send me presents at Christmas and birthdays. I might see her a few times on summer holiday. I must have made an impression on her, she could see that I had potential or whatever you call it."

"When was the last time you saw your aunt?" Inspector Crothers asked as he watched carefully for the man's reaction.

"When I got out of the can, she came to pick me up."

"You haven't seen her since?" the Inspector prodded.

"That's not right, I did see her last month. I needed some money, got myself in a bit of trouble with a local fellow, runs the bets here in Shrewsbury," Thomas said as he drained the beer out of the can in one gulp.

Sergeant Webster immediately responded, "You like to bet on the matches, is that it?"

"Always have, a weakness of mine. Football, cricket, rugby, I like them all, you don't mind if I have another one. Working at that shop is killing me, can't wait to move into that big old house, I am going to have a big flat-screen TV in every room, mark my words."

Inspector Crothers tried to overlook the man's callous attitude as he continued the questioning, "About the bets and money, how are your finances, do you owe anyone any money?"

"I've had a run of luck since I paid that guy off. Everything's been coming up roses for me, I pick the right teams and been doing good. If you don't think so, look at my aunt, just died and left me everything, how's that for luck? Must be my year."

"Your aunt didn't just die as you say, she was murdered in her home by someone she trusted, someone she was close to, and you think of that as lucky?" Sergeant Webster asked with barely concealed disgust.

"When you put it like that, it does sound rotten what I said. But here's the truth, I don't know why she left me everything but I'm glad she did. Working every day like a regular guy is not for me. It might be alright for you two gentlemen, working in a suit in a posh office, but not for me."

Sergeant Webster continued, "And her death? What about that? Doesn't it bother you that she was killed violently in her home by a person she knew, that she trusted?"

"It's terrible, that the old girl went out like that, but I didn't have nothing to do with it if that's what you mean. I was at work the day it happened, I know my rights and I got witnesses," Thomas insisted in a loud voice.

Inspector Crothers responded to the man's increasing agitation. "Mr. Tamarland, you are the sole beneficiary, you alone stand to gain from her death. You don't seem to have any remorse or sadness regarding her passing."

"Is that what you think? Because I didn't know her that well, because she left me everything and because I am not crying my eyes out, I must be guilty. Is it that or that I just got out of prison?" Thomas said as he gestured wildly with his beer.

"You have to admit that your record is not in your favor. You served time for swindling pensioners and then your aunt dies and leaves you every penny. If we didn't ask that question, how would that look? It would look like we weren't doing our jobs," said the Inspector, changing tactics.

Thomas Tamarland sighed, his demeanor less defensive. "You got a point when you put it like that, but this time I swear I didn't have a thing to do with it. What I did before was small-time, just a few hundred pounds here and there, nothing the old codgers would miss. But killing somebody was never my thing. You can ask anyone that knows me, I don't like fighting and I hate violence, except in rugby, but that's someone else breaking bones, not me."

Sergeant Webster played along with the Inspector. "Can you think of any information about your aunt that may be useful to us, anything about her life or her habits? I know you didn't spend time with her, but did she write you letters, call you, talk about her life?"

"Not anything you don't already know. My aunt kept to herself, she didn't like a lot of company even when I was a kid, it was quiet at her house, not a lot of noise or visitors. It was boring except she did let me watch the TV in the breakfast room and eat ice cream."

"Unless you can think of anything additional you would like to tell us, I believe our conversation is concluded for now," Inspector Crothers said as he stood up.

"Let me finish that for you, don't go anywhere, don't travel and don't leave town unless I check in with you gentlemen, is that right?" Thomas added with a smile.

"Yes, Mr. Tamarland, that's right, here is my card. We will be in touch," the Inspector answered.

"Look at the time, you did a good job, the match is coming on in a few minutes, looks like I won't have to miss a minute of it. Good thing too, I have a fiver riding on it."

"We will leave you to it, thank you Mr. Tamarland for your cooperation and I advise that you don't leave the county without contacting my office."

Inspector Crothers and Sergeant Webster left the squalor of the damp basement flat and walked back to the car. The Inspector removed his jacket and breathed in the fresh air. The rain was falling at a steady pace and he was getting wet as he stood by the car, but he didn't care and neither did Sergeant Webster, "I'm going to have to burn these clothes when I get home," Inspector Crothers said as he unlocked the car.

"I couldn't agree more, I need a hot shower and a shot of penicillin after being in that place. How does he live like that?"

"I shudder to think what Mrs. Tamarland's house is going to look like when he moves in. She was neat and tidy. She was a clean person and her nephew lives like that, she must have seen something in him that I'm missing."

"Or he was right and they weren't close, she may never have seen how the man lives."

Sergeant Webster looked down at the jacket folded over his arm as he slid into the passenger seat, "I'm going to miss this suit, it was one of my favorites."

Despite the rain, Inspector Crothers pushed the button on the door and rolled down the window of the driver's side, letting the smell of rain into the car, along with a few drops, before saying, "What do you think? He was one cool customer, wasn't he?"

"He sure was, but I just don't think he is our man, he works at an auto repair shop. I'll do the legwork on it, but he has the word of everyone that he works with that he was at the repair shop at the time of the murder, just like he said. If he called in sick or left early, we can find out about it, but I doubt it."

"What about the will, do you think he knew about it? Could he have convinced his aunt to mention him in the will?"

"That may be possible, but it doesn't look like a con job. He volunteered that information about owing money for gambling and betting. He didn't hesitate to say that he asked her for the money. If he was conning her, I don't think he would have given up that piece of information. Not willingly."

Inspector Crothers replied, "He's either the smartest criminal we have met in a long time or he is just as he seems, a small-time crook and con man with a gambling problem. He may have conned his aunt, but if she willingly left her entire estate to him, that isn't a crime, it's just poor judgment. I bet he spends every pound of it and sells the house in less than a year."

"Inspector, I know you told me that we would get something from the chippy after the interview, but I think I lost my appetite."

"Me too, I can't think about food after being in his flat. I hope he keeps his aunt's maid on to look after things at the house. I would hate to see the place condemned by a real estate inspector by the time he is through with it."

"Maid? You promised Diane that we would check into the maid. See what we could find out about her, do think we ought to pay her a visit?"

"I do want to talk to the maid, but not tonight, not wearing this suit that smells like the back room of a pub."

Sergeant Webster sniffed the jacket draped over his arm and threw it into the back seat, "It's probably too late for a visit and I need a shower before I go anywhere else."

Chapter 6

It was after eight when Inspector Crothers returned to his office He wanted to write the report about the interview with Thomas Tamarland while the details were still fresh in his mind. Powering on his computer, he quickly scanned his emails and was pleasantly surprised to see a message from the account manager of Mrs. Tamarland's bank. Opening the attachment to the file, he hit print. The printer spat out ten pages of banking history in less than a minute. As he scanned the documents, he was joined by Sergeant Webster.

"Are we working late tonight?" the Sergeant asked as he knocked on the open door of Inspector Crothers office.

"Hmmm?" Inspector Crothers answered as he read each line of the statements. "No I suppose not, you can go, I may be here for another hour."

"Two heads are better than one, I can stay," Sergeant Webster answered.

"In that case, read over these, make sure I haven't missed anything out of the ordinary."

"Yes sir, what would be out of the ordinary for Mrs. Tamarland? It's not like we know what is ordinary for her."

Inspector Crothers handed the Sergeant two pages from the statement as he answered, "One thing I can say for Mrs. Tamarland, she was organized and predictable. Her house was tidy, not a pillow out of place, her garden was weeded and in good order and her banking was just the same. From what I can tell by reading these statements, she paid the same bills every month, nothing out of the ordinary."

"Even recently, just before her death, was there anything unusual?" the Sergeant asked as he scanned the banking history.

"I have not read the recent statements yet," the Inspector said as he returned to his desk.

In only a few pages, he spotted an anomaly on the statement, a cheque that was written for 1500 pounds and cashed within a week of Mrs. Tamarland's death. "Sergeant, what do you make of this?" he asked as he showed the suspicious entry to Sergeant Webster.

"Let's see, I would say that is out of the ordinary. Did she make a purchase, a donation to charity perhaps, pay more of Thomas's debts than he admitted?"

Inspector Crothers turned his attention to the message on his computer, and saw an additional attachment that he'd neglected to print. Clicking the icon, he walked to the printer as the documents slid into the tray. Glancing at the pages, he quickly located the digital image of the cheque, "There it is, the recipient of the 1500 pounds," he said as he handed the page to the Sergeant.

Sergeant Webster looked at the cheque as he said, "Ruth Hedley, that's the maid's name, isn't it?"

"Yes, it is, I would say that is out of the ordinary for Mrs. Tamarland."

"Could it be a bonus, a gift, what about a loan?" asked the Sergeant.

"It may be, but that is a large sum of money for an employer to give a woman that comes in to clean the house once a week, especially just before that employer ends up dead in her own home days later. I will contact the account manager tomorrow morning for the details but I doubt he can answer our questions. Sergeant, you and Diane are right, it is time we paid the maid a visit."

Chapter 7

"A cheque for 1500 pounds? That is a lot of money," Diane replied as she powered off her laptop, "Were there any other cheques like that written out of the account or to the maid?"

Light filtered through the limbs of the oak tree overhead, shading Diane and the Inspector as they sat at the wrought iron table in the garden. Their conversation centered on the latest development in the Tamarland case.

Temporarily distracted by the view of the roses and the water fountain, the Inspector hesitated before he answered Diane's question, "No, that was the only one in the banking history. There were one or two cheques that were cashed for a couple hundred pounds over the years made out to Mrs. Hedley, but this one was unique in the amount."

Diane nodded her head as she asked, "Inspector, do you think that Mrs. Tamarland wrote it? Is it possible that the maid stole a blank cheque, wrote in the amount that she needed and cashed it, hoping that her employer wouldn't notice?"

Inspector Crothers smiled at Diane as he said, "It never ceases to amaze me how much you and I think alike. I had the same thought but the account manager provided digital copies of the cheques that Mrs. Tamarland wrote every month and the handwriting and signature match."

"Perhaps the maid forged the handwriting?"

"That is always a possibility but unlikely. According to the account manager, Mrs. Tamarland kept a close watch on her accounts and was not the least bit surprised that 1500 pounds was paid to her maid."

"It is still strange that the cheque cleared her account a few days before her death."

"I agree, which is why Sergeant Webster and I are going to pay Mrs. Hedley a visit this afternoon."

"What about the nephew, have you uncovered anything that might lead to an arrest?"

Inspector Crothers involuntarily shuddered at the mention of the nephew. "Thomas Tamarland is still on my list of possible suspects."

"The interview with him, what happened?"

"He was cavalier about his aunt's death, unapologetic about his gambling problem and lives in squalor. He is also one of the calmest suspects I have interviewed in my career. In my experience, even innocent people are nervous around me when I start asking questions."

Diane frowned. "He sounds unsavory, but do you think he killed his aunt or had anything to do with her murder?"

"He seems like the type, a con man that swindles pensioners finally striking it big, but I don't have any solid evidence that places him at her house at the time of her death. At this stage in the investigation, I am not ruling him out."

"Honestly, Inspector, do you think he hired someone to do it? He could have lied about his knowledge of the contents of the will, promising to pay the killer a hefty sum?"

Inspector Crothers rubbed his chin, a gesture that Diane noticed he did when he was deep in thought.

After a few minutes of silence, he answered, "My first impression of Thomas is that he is a loner, doesn't like to share or work with others. However, Mrs. Tamarland left him a small fortune which might have changed things. He may have been willing to share a cut to get his hands on it. It would be the biggest payout of his career and for that he may have been willing to branch out of his comfort zone and hire someone that didn't mind violence."

"I hope you don't mind that I did a little nosing around town. Regrettably, I haven't uncovered a single piece of useful information. Everyone liked Mrs. Tamarland but didn't know a lot about her. I didn't uncover one shred of gossip or even a negative remark. Her life was as it appeared, quiet, orderly and predictable."

"Which leaves us with the interview this afternoon with the maid. I am counting on it. If she can provide some insight into Mrs. Tamarland's life or proves to be a suspect, we may be able to solve this case. Whether it is the nephew or the maid, what we know is that someone sat down to tea with the woman and then shot her to death, Mrs. Hedley was with her once a week, maybe she knows something we don't," Inspector Crothers said as he stood to leave.

"I hope so," Diane replied as she turned the computer on. "What about forensics, anything that we may have missed? What do you know about the gun used in the murder?"

"All the evidence indicates an older gun – most likely from the Second World War. This might indicate an old solder from that war, or at least somebody who might have lived with such a person."

"Did they turn up anything else of interest?"

"There isn't much to report on that end, just a few strands of hair from the couch."

"Hair? What kind of hair?" asked Diane.

"Canine."

"Mrs. Tamarland didn't have any pets, could that be a clue?"

"I wouldn't put too much stock in it, someone she knew may have a dog. Finding canine and feline hair are common to any investigation," Inspector Crothers said, dismissively. "I will keep you posted."

Diane waved to Inspector Crothers as he left the garden. This case was proving to be frustrating; every new clue turned into a dead end. Turning her attention back to her work, she tried to concentrate on the flashing cursor on the blank screen in front of her, but her mind was consumed by the facts of the case, facts that were not leading to an arrest. With her hands on the keyboard of the laptop, the cursor blinking at her, she tried to remain optimistic that Inspector Crothers would learn something useful when he spoke with Mrs. Hedley.

Chapter 8

Inspector Crothers drove down the lane headed back to the station. The afternoon interview with Mrs. Hedley was the biggest lead in the case. Mrs. Hedley worked for Mrs. Tamarland for several years and was the one person that might be able to shed some light on the secretive life of the victim. If the maid didn't have any relevant information, he was going to be stuck at a dead end. When he thought of Mrs. Tamarland and the cold-blooded way she met her end, he felt that he owed it to her, owed the community by solving her murder.

Returning to his office, he was met by Sergeant Webster, his jacket in his hand. "I finished the witness statements. Thomas was at work the day of the murder, just like he said. His co-workers and his boss gave detailed testimony. He doesn't like to work, but they all saw him that afternoon, in the break room or smoking a cigarette."

"They are willing to testify that he was being lazy, is that it?" asked Inspector Crothers.

"You are right on the mark, according to his boss there is a security camera on the premises. He volunteered to provide footage of that afternoon if it was necessary."

"Not at this stage of the investigation," answered the Inspector as he glanced at his watch. "We'd better get going if we want to make that appointment with Mrs. Hedley."

Sergeant Webster slipped on his jacket, "I am ready to go when you are."

Mrs. Ruth Hedley did not live in Apple Mews, but in the nearby town of Tynemouth on Haye, a quiet hamlet nestled on a river. As Inspector Crothers drove through the town, he was struck by the scenic beauty of the small village. "Sergeant, this place makes Apple Mews look like a bustling metropolis."

"It looks like a travel poster for Shropshire, every building is historic and every garden well-tended," Sergeant Webster replied. "Look at that church, will you? It has to be a few hundred years old and that pub probably saw a lot of history."

"I don't know why there aren't tourists swarming all over this place," Inspector Crothers said as he turned the car down a narrow street.

"They just don't know about it, is all. I've lived in Shropshire all my life and I can't say that I can recall having a reason to come here."

Inspector Crothers parked in front of a row of clean but small two-story houses. The street was barely wide enough to allow for parked cars and traffic. As he stepped out of the vehicle and stood on the cobblestone street, he estimated that the road beneath his feet, like the houses, dated back a few centuries.

"It's a nice little street, there isn't much to it, but it's clean, the houses all look well kept," said Sergeant Webster as they walked up the front steps of a narrow single-family dwelling.

The Inspector pushed the button on the door frame, and a doorbell cheerfully rang inside the modest home. A dog barked a high-pitched warning from somewhere behind the door.

"Sounds like a yippy little dog," whispered the Inspector.

"'Bet it's an ankle biter, what do you think, a tiny dog that thinks he's a wolfhound?" Sergeant Webster replied as the door slowly opened, revealing a middle-aged woman.

"May I help you?" she said as she squinted at the men on her doorstep, her face softening into a friendly expression as she recognized Crothers and Webster. "Inspector, please forgive me, I can't see without my glasses."

A diminutive mixed-breed dog stood shaking behind its owner. Its teeth bared, it was growling and barking its displeasure at the intruders on its well-guarded perimeter.

"Sampson! Go lie down, don't wake daddy up, you hear me?" the woman said in a low voice.

The little dog bowed its head as it growled, "You will have to excuse Sampson, he gets excited when we have visitors, he won't hurt you, he is all bark," she assured the officers as she reached into the pocket of her apron and pulled out a pair of glasses held together by tape. "That's better, please, come in. I've just put the kettle on."

"Has he had all his shots?" asked the Sergeant as he eyed the dog warily.

"Oh my, yes, he gets more trips to the doctor than I do, please come in."

Ruth Hedley was a middle-aged woman with wiry gray hair crammed into a bun at the back of her head. The glasses on her face gave her a faint resemblance to a well-fed pigeon, the Inspector observed as he followed her to the sitting room.

"Have a seat. I was expecting you, I have biscuits and tea, but I can make sandwiches if you prefer," she replied as the little dog lay in the doorway, its gaze fixed on the strangers in its house.

"Thank you, Mrs. Hedley. We are on duty and don't want to be a bother. We regret that we must decline your hospitality," Inspector Crothers said as he sat down on the narrow couch.

"I understand, I have never been interviewed by the police before and I didn't know what I should do, tea always seems like a good idea for guests."

"It was very nice of you," said the Sergeant with a smile.

Mrs. Ruth Hedley sat on a well-worn upholstered chair in the modest sitting room of her home. A fireplace was the prominent feature of the room that was immaculately clean and sported family photographs in frames carefully arranged on the mantle. The furniture, like the rug on the floor, looked as though it had seen better days, but had been kept clean. Inspector Crothers did not see a single cobweb or speck of dust anywhere in the room, a detail that illustrated the pride she had in her home and her work.

"I hope you will excuse the mess, it is so hard to keep my own house clean and work the hours I do," she apologized.

"Mrs. Hedley, there is no need to apologize, we are not home inspectors and if we were, I would give you the highest marks," said Inspector Crothers as he tried to ease into the questioning that was to follow.

"Thank you for that," she said with a faint smile. "I know you didn't drive all this way for an afternoon chat, what can I do to help you? Mrs. Tamarland was my favorite employer and I will do anything I can to help you find the person responsible for what happened to her," she said as she removed her glasses and wiped her eyes with her hand.

"Mrs. Hedley, before we discuss Mrs. Tamarland, can you tell us something about you, just a few details for the record," Inspector Crothers asked to begin the interview.

Mrs. Hedley looked uncomfortable as she bit her lip and wrung her hands together, "There isn't much to tell that you don't know. I am married, have been for nearly thirty years now. My husband, Eddie, is a pipe fitter when he can find work."

She quickly glanced towards the ceiling as she spoke, "There hasn't been much work for him these last few years, which is why I'm cleaning houses and doing odd jobs for people. I do a bit of mending and sewing from time to time to make ends meet too."

From the woman's statement to Sampson dog and her habit of looking up at the second floor, Sergeant

Webster realized that Eddie Hedley was upstairs. Lowering his voice, he asked, "Has it been difficult to make ends meet in the last few weeks?"

Her cheeks turned crimson as she stammered. From the kitchen, the kettle whistled startling her, "Oh dear, I better get that. I don't want Eddie to wake up, he needs his sleep."

Jumping up from the chair, she moved surprisingly fast for a woman her age, Inspector Crothers noted as he watched her.

She returned to the sitting room, exasperated and anxious as she sat down. Glancing at the ceiling once more, she looked at the Sergeant as she answered in a whisper, "You asked me about making ends meet, yes, it has been hard the last two months, with Eddie out of a regular job. He has had a few part-time jobs but nothing to amount to very much lately."

Inspector Crothers asked the question that was burning in his mind, "Is that why Mrs. Tamarland wrote you that cheque?"

"I was afraid you would ask me about that, please don't say another word about it, I don't want Eddie to know," she whispered, "He would be furious with me for asking one of my employers for money."

"He doesn't know about it?" Sergeant Webster asked, quietly.

"No, no one but you two, the bank and Mrs. Tamarland, God rest her soul, knew about it. It's in a savings account that has my name on it, he doesn't know about it and I pray he never does. With that money, I can keep a roof over our heads for a few more months until he goes back to work."

Inspector Crothers continued, "I will make this as quick as I can, was it a loan or a gift?"

Mrs. Hedley looked uncomfortable as she shifted in her chair, "I told her it was a loan, like the ones before. I always managed to pay her back, even if it meant I had to work twice as hard. But this time, I don't suppose I have to pay it back, do I? That is not nice to say, is it?"

"The truth can be like that sometimes. Since you don't have to pay it back, that must be a relief to you," said Sergeant Webster.

"Sir, I didn't mean it like that, honest. I adored Mrs. Tamarland, she was a sweet, gentle woman and she took pity on me. I only meant that if I don't have to pay it back, that I wouldn't have to work so hard. With her death, I lost one of my best-paying employers and I am going to feel that loss of pay, I just know it. Finding someone like her is going to be hard in these parts."

Sergeant Webster lowered his voice, "I don't mean to ask this of you, but I have to know for the record, why is your husband unable to work?"

Mrs. Hedley blushed as she pursed her lips together, pausing before answering the question, "He has not been up to the work, he has been unwell."

"Unwell? Is he under a doctor's care?"

Ruth Hedley shook her head and mouthed the word, "No."

Inspector Crothers tried to be tactful as he asked, "Is it an illness or something else that has made you the sole breadwinner in the house?"

"I don't talk about it, but," she said in a whisper, "it's something else. Please don't ask me about it."

Inspector Crothers did not pursue the truth about Eddie. Unknown to Mrs. Hedley, it was only a temporary reprieve from a painful conversation. He changed the subject as he asked, "Mrs. Hedley, can you tell us anything about Mrs. Tamarland, any family members, any visitors or friends she may have invited to her house?"

"Inspector, sir, there is not much to tell about her. She kept to herself, went to church, she liked to garden. You should see her roses, I told her they needed to be entered into one of those competitions."

Sergeant Webster gently prodded the maid, "Mrs. Hedley, there must have been someone she spoke to, her nephew perhaps?"

Ruth Hedley's pleasant demeanor changed at the mention of Thomas Tamarland. She frowned as she answered, "What? Him? He wasn't worth her time if you ask me. I know it isn't my place to say a word about her relations but that man was in prison, though you already know that. Mrs. Tamarland told me and swore me not to tell a soul. She left her money and her fine house to him."

"Did he coerce her in any way, make her add him to the will?" asked the Inspector.

"If he did, I didn't see it or hear about it. I think she felt sorry for him. She was kind-hearted like that, same as she did with me, although I always paid her back until this last time."

Inspector Crothers looked intently at Mrs. Hedley as he said, "Mrs. Hedley, you were the only member of her staff, possibly her closest friend, you must have known who she was having tea with the afternoon of her death. In a life as private as hers, she must have mentioned the arrival of a visitor."

Ruth Hedley shook her head as she answered, "I have racked my brain every moment since I found Mrs. Tamarland on the rug, dead." Mrs. Hedley's voice cracked as she continued, "I should have known who did this to her, have some idea but I don't. I didn't know she was having anyone to tea, I never heard her mention plans to have a guest to the house."

"Were there any unusual phone calls, or letters?" asked Sergeant Webster.

"I only came in once a week, if she received an odd phone call I may not have known about it. The letters and mail she kept in her desk in the study or upstairs at the antique writing desk in her bedroom."

Inspector Crothers looked at the Sergeant, "Unless you have any further questions for Mrs. Hedley, I think we are done here."

Sergeant Webster answered, "No, none that come to mind."

"Mrs. Hedley, thank you for your time, please contact me if you remember any information that may help. We will be in touch," Inspector Crothers said as he handed his card to the woman.

"Yes sir, I will," she said as she walked the officers to the door.

Inspector Crothers and Sergeant Webster were quiet on the drive back to the office, until Sergeant Webster broke the silence, "Since it can't hurt anything to have one more look, I may inspect the letters and mail Mrs. Hedley was talking about. We might have missed something the first time around."

"That is not a bad idea, Sergeant, what did you make of Mrs. Hedley?"

"Mrs. Hedley? She seemed like a sweet lady, her house was neat as a pin and I bet you anything she can cook. What do you think about the husband?"

"That is hard to say but she acted nervous every time she mentioned him. I may be wrong, but she is hiding something about him and possibly more than that."

"Hiding something, that dear old woman?"

"She was a textbook kindly old lady, offered to make us tea, had a small dog, kept a perfect house. It could all be an act."

"I just don't buy it, she seemed so real."

"You are probably right, but there is a clue in this case that we are missing and until I find what that is, I am going to assume that nothing is as it appears. The murderer must have left us a scrap of evidence to go on and we are not seeing it."

As Inspector Crothers parked the car, his mobile phone vibrated in his pocket. He turned off the vehicle as he answered the call, "Crothers here."

Sergeant Webster could not hear the conversation but he watched as the Inspector's face tightened into a deep scowl.

"Yes sir, we just got back, we are walking in the office now." The Inspector powered off the phone and let out a deep sigh that sounded like a rush of air.

"Inspector?"

"Webster, you won't believe this, but we have another one."

"Another one, sir?"

"Another murder, this one is in that idyllic village we just left. The victim was Mrs. Cranston Buxby, she was over sixty, widowed and lived alone."

Chapter 9

The Shrewsbury Daily Post sat on a silver tray, folded neatly at the breakfast table. The headline *Retired Bank Employee Found Dead* printed in a bold large font was clearly visible in Diane's peripheral vision as she drank her first cup of tea of the day. She did not need to reach for the newspaper, as she already knew the details of the latest unsolved murder, a luxury few people in Apple Mews could claim.

The second unsolved murder in less than a month was not just unsettling to Diane, but to everyone in her acquaintance. The mood had changed in the quiet village of Apple Mews; tea shops that were once bustling centers of community news and local gossip had become hotbeds of fear and speculation. Villagers were locking their doors at night and checking their windows, retirees were sleeping with the lights on and refusing to venture out in the evening. The town was living in fear, especially women living alone.

Mrs. Cranston Buxby was not from Apple Mews, but she was from a village in Shropshire and that was all the connection that the population of Apple Mews needed to justify their growing anxiety. Two women, both widows, both living alone were dead, their murders unsolved. That was enough justification to warrant a growing demand that something, anything be done.

As Diane picked at the egg white omelet on her plate, she dreaded to think the unthinkable, that the murderer was targeting retired women, an unsettling thought as she herself had only recently fallen into the very same category.

Albert finished his cup of tea as he watched his wife fretting over her breakfast, "Any word from the Inspector this morning?"

Diane shook her head, "Not yet."

"I would not want to be in his shoes today, Mrs. Tamarland's murder left unsolved and now this one, the public will be demanding answers soon."

"They already are, have you seen the editorial pages in the papers this week? I can't bear to read it."

"Diane, do you think the public is being rash? Jumping to conclusions, there doesn't seem to be much connecting the two victims; one lived in Apple Mews the other in Tynemouth on Haye."

"You know I am not prone to hysterics, but Albert, those women could have been me, they could have been any one of our friends or neighbors."

"I understand, I do, but there isn't much of a connection. Didn't you say that the lady, Mrs. Buxby, was poisoned?"

"She was poisoned, found in her home by a concerned neighbor."

"Inspector Crothers is here to see you," Deidre announced to Diane as she walked into the breakfast room.

"Show him to the drawing room," Diane said as she turned to Albert. "It must be important for the Inspector to make an appearance this early in the day."

"From the looks of things, I would say that he needs all the help he can manage," Albert answered.

Diane left the breakfast room and joined Inspector Crothers in the drawing room. The dark circles around the Inspector's eyes and wrinkled suit gave Diane the distinct impression that he had not slept or been home to change clothes. He looked haggard, with a frown set on his face as he greeted Diane.

"Please excuse the intrusion at this early hour, I would not have come but I need to speak with you."

"There is nothing to excuse, Inspector. I know I've said this to you before, but you look exhausted."

He broke into a smile as he looked down at his clothes. "I look terrible, but that is not important, not when we have a killer on the loose."

Diane was not accustomed to hearing dire comments and dramatic statements being spouted by a man she knew to be reliable, steadfast and stoic. His tone matched the hysteria in the village and she wondered if it was a product of his lack of sleep that was creating the rash judgment he voiced.

"Inspector," Diane said as she fought the rising anxiety she also felt, "Mrs. Tamarland was shot in Apple Mews. Mrs. Buxby was poisoned in Tynemouth on Haye. Do you believe that they were both killed by the same person?"

"Diane, I never like to rush to conclusions, but can you tell me that you don't believe there is a connection? The evidence is mounting that we may have a serial killer in our midst."

Diane decided that the best course of action was to review the facts of the new case. "Let's not speculate, let's focus only on the facts. You have not slept in more than day or two, you must have been busy, what have you learned about the death of Mrs. Buxby?"

"It was poison, obviously and irrefutably poison. I have seen poison cases in the past, but rarely have I ever seen one as brazen as this one. The murderer did not take any great pains to cover up the cause of death."

"How was it administered?"

"The coroner seems to think the poison was in food or drink, although there doesn't seem to be any residue or sign of poison in the residence, and believe me we have combed every room in the house, especially the kitchen."

"Tell me about the poison, what do you know about it?"

"That is what makes this so frustrating. The poison itself appeared to be similar to a painkiller, a morphine-based compound with a twist, arsenic may have been added."

"That sounds like a potent cocktail."

"The presence of the poison would be obvious in an autopsy," Inspector Crothers replied. "That is one of the reasons why these two cases seem connected. It's not only what the victims have in common that begs the conclusion that they are connected, but the same cavalier method of murder. In both cases, the murderer was not concerned with concealment of the crime."

"There was no evidence of a theft, nothing missing?"

"All valuables and personal possessions were present at Mrs. Buxby's home, her purse was found on the sofa, the car keys lying beside it. The home was in good order, nothing appeared disorganized."

The Inspector and Diane sat in silence, deep in thought. Diane could feel the weight of the responsibility to the other women in Shropshire to find the killer before there was a third murder to discuss. Her mind was racing, going in a thousand directions, each one leading to a dead end.

"Once again, if you will indulge me, Inspector. May I go over the facts that we know about Mrs. Buxby? The facts help me see the case clearly."

"Yes, very well."

"Mrs. Buxby was a retired secretary, she worked for the president of Midlands Banking and Trust, she lived alone in Tynemouth on Haye. She was in her sixties, widowed and had one child, is that correct?"

"It is, the daughter, Mrs. Alice Buxby Upton, lives in Leeds, married to a prominent business owner."

Diane continued with the facts of the case, "The neighbors did not report any unusual activity, her banking records are devoid of any suspicious transactions, her will seems to be in order."

"Precisely, she lived a nice, neat, predictable life. She went to church, was a member of the local gardening club and popped over to Leeds now and again to see her daughter."

"Retired, predictable and now dead, just like Mrs. Tamarland. Do we have any information about her social activities? Was she dating, did she have friends, was she involved in community service?" asked Diane as she tried to find a promising lead.

"She was not seeing anyone, or if she was she kept the fact to herself. Her friends were like her, retired, and she was active in her community, volunteering at her church for charity events."

"She sounds like Mrs. Tamarland, only slightly more social," Diane remarked. "Is there any possibility that she and Mrs. Tamarland may have known each other, they both shared a penchant for church charity events?"

"Good idea, but different churches, Mrs. Buxby attended church in Tynemouth on Haye."

"Tynemouth on Haye," repeated Diane, "Mrs. Tamarland's maid lives in Tynemouth, does she not?"

"She does, but Mrs. Buxby did not employ a maid."

"It is a small village, smaller than Apple Mews, perhaps they knew each other socially? Is it possible that Mrs. Hedley is the connection you have been looking for?"

"I can't say that thought has not crossed my mind, but a retired bank secretary and a maid would have frequented different social circles even in a tiny village."

"If these women followed conventional social norms, that may have been the case. They may have known each other, gone to school together. What about their husbands, any affiliations between Mr. Tamarland or Mr. Buxby?"

"Mr. Tamarland, as you may know, was from Apple Mews, Mr. Buxby was from a village in Kent. I have not discovered a connection or affiliation between the two husbands."

Diane continued in her task, trying to find the detail that would lead to the killer. "Mrs. Hedley has a dog and you found canine hair at Mrs. Tamarland's home. Was there any hair found in Mrs. Buxby's residence? Did she have any pets, did you find any dog hair?"

"She did not have any pets and we did not find any canine hair, although there were a few strands of feline hair in the carpet in the hallway, suggesting someone she knew has a cat."

Diane could feel in her gut that there was something just beyond her knowledge. She knew there had to be something connecting the two women in some way, some detail that she was overlooking. Rarely had a case frustrated her, but this one was beginning to worm its way under her skin.

"Not to sound too glaringly obvious, but Thomas Tamarland did not have a connection to Mrs. Buxby, though Mrs. Hedley living in the same village might have known both women."

"It is possible, Tynemouth on Haye is that kind of place."

"Tell me Inspector, the poison was slow acting and you have not had any luck whatsoever finding evidence that it was introduced inside her home. The neighbors did not report any strange visitors or unusual activity. You may be too narrow in your area of concentration."

The Inspector frowned as he asked, "Too narrow, what do you mean?"

"The house was clean, nothing disorganized you said, yet Mrs. Buxby's purse was left on the sofa, her keys lying beside it. That seems strange, for a person as neat and predictable as she was, she would have had a place for her purse and her keys other than the sofa."

The Inspector's eyes lit up. "I did not think of that, for all we know she may have always left her purse on the sofa, but it doesn't fit with the housekeeping in the rest of her residence. The clothes in her closet were sorted by color, her shoes in neat rows, the dishes in her kitchen were carefully lined in rows inside the cabinets, Diane, you may be on to something."

"Regarding her clothes, was she dressed casually for an afternoon at home, or was she dressed to have been on errands or paying a social call?"

"I am not an expert in fashion, but she was wearing shoes suitable for outdoors, a cotton twill pair of pants and a lightweight sweater if that helps."

"Any jewelry?"

"Yes, now that you mention it, a watch on her left arm, a pair of gold earrings and a small gold pendant."

"Inspector, she was dressed to go out, which proves my theory that the poison was not administered at her residence. If she was suffering from the effects of a morphine-based poison, she may have been poisoned somewhere else and managed to make it home before she died. Depending on the severity of the symptoms, you may find that her car may not be parked properly, her front door left unlocked, that sort of thing."

"Her car was parked at an odd angle, the driver-side back tire wedged against the curb, the car was turned off in drive and not park. I noticed those details, but I thought she was in a hurry or a terrible driver. The front door of her home was unlocked when the neighbor came to check on her when her body was found."

"I would wager that she knew her killer and met that person earlier on the day of her death. If you can establish an exact time of death and an estimation of how long it took before the poison went into effect, you may have a solid lead. I do not mean to be indelicate, but the contents of her last meal may be a good indicator of where that meeting could have taken place if such a meeting occurred. It would align with the evidence that coroner suggested that the poison was administered in food or drink."

"That is not much to go on, but it's a start, thank you Diane."

"Inspector, one more thing, don't forget Mrs. Hedley. It seems odd, but she may be a connection."

"I will check into it, you have my word. Diane, thank you for your help," Inspector Crothers said as he stood to leave.

"Anytime, let me know what you find out."

"I will, you can be sure of that."

"One last thing. Try to get a few hours rest, at least change your clothes, you will feel better," Diane said with a sympathetic smile.

Chapter 10

Inspector Crothers left Diane's house with a sense of reluctant optimism. In his present exhausted state, he was aware that his thinking about the case was dulled by fatigue. He needed rest, but the public and his own sense of duty were keeping him from slowing down long enough to sleep. The day ahead was going to be a long one, but Diane was right, he needed rest. Yawning as he pulled out of the driveway, he should have headed for the office but instead, he headed for home. An hour's nap and a quick shower would do him an enormous amount of good.

It was quarter past eleven when Inspector Crothers walked into his office; his face was freshly shaved, and he was sporting a fresh suit. The circles around his eyes were still dark reminders of his lack of rest, but he felt better, calmer. Sergeant Webster was in Tynemouth on Haye, his job being to dig up any information about Mrs. Buxby that could be useful.

Inspector Crothers reached into his pocket and checked for messages, though did not see any waiting as he called the coroner's office. He was pleased that the coroner was available for a quick chat. As Inspector Crothers listened to the coroner's detailed explanation of the inner workings of the human digestive tract and how long it takes food to digest or break down in a living subject versus a dead one, he felt mildly queasy. He had seen stabbings, gunshot wounds and much worse during his days in the army and on the police force, but any conversation with the coroner always managed to turn his stomach.

The coroner was not able to provide the exact breakdown of Mrs. Buxby's last meal but it appeared to be dense like cake or bread, and a high amount of caffeine was found in the toxicology report. Mrs. Buxby's time of death after the poison entered her system was approximately two to three hours. The coroner also suggested that the poison being morphine based may have caused Mrs. Buxby to exhibit symptoms as early as an hour after ingesting it. He further suggested that the painkillers may have masked some of the arsenic's nastier side effects.

Inspector Crothers thanked the coroner and walked to the break room, sliding his phone into his pocket as he walked down the narrow corridor. After that conversation, he needed a strong cup of tea. Halfway down the corridor, he stopped what he was doing and immediately turned around, rushing back to his office. Tea - that was it, there was another detail the two victims had in common. He could not be certain, but if the coroner was correct, Mrs. Buxby's last meal could have been tea. The contents of her stomach and the caffeine in her bloodstream all pointed to it.

Switching on his computer at his desk, he accessed the messages and scrolled to the bank records of Mrs. Buxby. Clicking on the file of her recent transaction history, he scrolled down the debits and credits of her chequeing account searching for the hours leading to her death. His eyes fell on the date of her death. It appeared that Mrs. Buxby had been busy that day; her debit card purchases tracked her activities. Before lunch, there was a modest purchase of petrol in Tynemouth on Haye, a purchase of groceries, and three hours later a visit to a local pharmacist.

Inspector Crothers looked at the transactions. These were the last hours of Mrs. Buxby's life staring at him. He felt like he was on the verge of making the discovery that would crack the case. Peering at the screen, he thought about the three hours between the grocery store and the pharmacist. It was in those three hours that she had met her killer, ingested the poison. He decided to pay a visit to Tynemouth on Haye, as he wanted to speak to the pharmacist.

Walking to his car, he remembered that he had not stopped for a cup of tea. Tea, it was the social glue that held the nation together, it was the one meal that strangers, acquaintances and old friends could gather as equals over. As he slid into the driver's seat he thought of Mrs. Hedley offering to make tea. She lived in Tynemouth on Haye, not far from the shops, if his memory served correctly.

His afternoon was going to be busy, and he needed a cup of tea. As he headed to the village nestled on the banks of the Haye, he suspected there was a tea shop in the village, a tea shop that he hoped would have a good strong cup of tea and a few answers to go along with it. If the tea shop didn't hold the answers he was looking for, he would pay a friendly call on a certain Mrs. Hedley, a woman who would undoubtedly offer him a cup of tea.

Chapter 11

Diane was frustrated. There was nothing about this case that was falling into place easily. Two women, over the age of sixty, were dead, both victims of foul play. The women lived in Shropshire, led quiet lives, and shared an interest in charity and little else. Sitting in the garden, an untouched cup of tea on the table at her side, Diane wrote the facts of both cases in a notepad.

As a murder mystery writer, she often outlined the plot of her books using this old-fashioned method of pen and paper, eschewing all modern technology. There was something almost meditative in the act of writing down the details of a case. As Diane stared at the notes written in her neat cursive, she could feel that an obvious clue was staring at her from the page. This clue, this elusive fact she was missing, and so was the Inspector.

They were getting closer to finding the lead, she could feel it, but it was still evading them, like a name on the tip of a tongue. The victims both enjoyed a last meal of tea, both knew the murderer, that was a connection, but it could have also been a coincidence. Was there anything else that may have connected them in a way that neither she nor the Inspector were able to discern?

Was it the maid, Mrs. Hedley, or could it be something else?

While Inspector Crothers was spending the afternoon in Tynemouth on Haye, Diane was compelled to spend her time also gainfully employed in the pursuit of the killer, but the question was, how should she pursue a lead when she was left without one? Diane reached for the cup of tea, found it cold but chose to drink it. Cold tea was better than no tea, and she hated to be wasteful. Putting the teacup back on the saucer, she considered the cold tea, and a thought entered her mind that was so unbelievably simple that it nearly made her laugh out loud like a mad woman.

"Cold," she said to herself as she drank the last sip of the tea from the cup, "that may be it!"

Jumping to her feet, she rushed inside the house, hoping to find her husband still at home. He was due at an emergency meeting of the village council in Apple Mews. Diane prayed he had not slipped out of the house without his customary goodbye kiss before he left.

"Albert!" she called out as she raced upstairs.

"Yes, my dear, whatever is the matter?" he said as he stepped into the hallway.

"What time is your meeting?"

"In less than an hour, why? You look upset, are you well?"

"I am very well, Albert, I can't believe I didn't see it before," she answered as she beamed at her husband.

"See what?"

"We have been looking in the wrong place. Mrs. Tamarland and Mrs. Buxby were retired, they were our age, don't you see? We have been looking at the wrong set of facts!"

"My dear, you do realize that I am incapable of following your train of thought, sit down and tell me what you have discovered."

Albert urged Diane to sit on the edge of the bed, then sat beside her as he said, "There, that's better."

"We have been looking at their lives in the present tense, focusing on who they knew just before their death, investigating their activities and their present financial circumstances. Don't you see, Albert? That may have been the mistake; these women all died at our age and our mistake has been believing that something in their present was the cause, but what if it was a connection from their past, something that these women were involved in when they were younger, in their twenties or forties? Is it possible they have a shared past, like a cold case, unsolved and forgotten for decades?"

Albert nodded his head as he stared at his wife. "You may be right. When I look back at my past and the number of people I have met over the years, it only stands to reason that these women may be the victims of someone they knew many years ago."

"Precisely, like an old friend, or acquaintance, someone they knew, someone they would enjoy catching up with over tea."

Diane could feel it, the lead she sought for so long was right there, she just had to find a place to begin. As her mind raced, she knew that she needed somewhere to begin the search. Two women were dead, a killer was on the loose and the village of Apple Mews was gripped by fear, as evidenced by the meeting that Albert was due to attend that afternoon, the subject of which was the security of the residents.

Diane sat on the edge of the bed as Albert opened the closet and selected a jacket. Mrs. Buxby was outgoing; her work as a bank secretary and her involvement in the garden club meant that she probably had a wide range of acquaintances. As Diane thought of forty years' worth of her own friends and neighbors, the task ahead of her was daunting. She needed to find a way to narrow down her search. As she watched Albert she remembered a detail that she overlooked. Mrs. Tamarland was a client of Albert's, she was reclusive, which would limit her circle of friends and acquaintances. If there was a connection, someone both women may have known, the person would be easier to spot in Mrs. Tamarland's past.

"Albert, Mrs. Tamarland was a client of yours for years, she carried your card in her purse, what do you make of that?"

"I would say that she must have been pleased with the firm."

"Very pleased to have considered your firm important enough to carry your card with her."

"I consider it a compliment," he said with a smile.

"Yes, I do too, but it may also be proof of how few people she considered friends. I was wondering if we could look at her files. There may be mention of a relation or a person that she might have known in her past."

"She is deceased, the only matter left to settle is the will, I don't see why not. I could drop you off at the office while I'm at the meeting."

"I have to be honest, I don't know what I am looking for, but I know you and your staff. I am counting on your attention to detail in this case."

"I don't want to discourage you but Mrs. Tamarland was the quiet sort, I am not sure what you will find."

"Albert, I honestly don't know what else I can do. All I know is that our methods for locating the killer aren't working and your firm has a connection to her that extends into her past. I agree it's tenuous, but it's a place to begin."

Chapter 12

An hour later Diane sat in a conference room of Albert's law firm, a box of old files beside her. She sneezed as she pulled decades' worth of paperwork pertaining to Mrs. Tamarland from the box, disturbing the fine layer of dust. A notepad and a pen sat in front of her, her mobile phone silent on the table. She did not want to inform Inspector Crothers of her activities until she had something substantial that he could use. As she opened the first file, she came to the realization that this was not going to be quick or painless. She had years of legal documents and notes to search; the clue, if it was in there, was going to remain hidden unless she was thorough in her search.

Diane was unaware of the passage of time as she meticulously examined every note, every word regarding Mrs. Tamarland. Stifling a yawn, she was unaware that she had spent the better part of two hours reviewing paperwork that stretched back several decades. Albert returned from his meeting, a cup of tea in his hand.

"I thought you might need this," he said with a smile as he set the tea down on the table.

Diana looked up from the file she was reading, rubbing her eyes. She saw the tea and her face lit up. "How wonderful, I needed a cup of tea."

"I thought you might, how is the search going?"

"Slow, I haven't found anything really useful but then again, I have never been one for tedious legal documents regarding ownership of property and other documents of the sort."

"Strange," Albert said as he reached for a file inside the box, "I never cared for legal documents either. I am fortunate I had a good staff I could rely on to supply the reams of paperwork that were required for even the simplest of cases."

"Reams of paperwork is right, that is all I have been reading since you left me. I haven't come across a single interesting note or document."

"It's not surprising, these files are just the history of any property Mrs. Tamarland or her husband may have bought or sold," Albert said as he flipped through the files. "These are not the complete files. Her late husband's will and her own would have been filed separately, I will get those files for you."

Albert soon returned with a stack of files. Handing them to his wife, he said, "Here we are, you may find this reading to be less tedious. You read through these and I will continue to search the property files. If I see anything interesting I will let you know."

"Thank you, two sets of eyes are better than one."

Albert sat down at the table beside Diane as she pored over the paperwork regarding the will. Digging into the box, he removed a file commenting, "How strange, this is a civil matter, what is it doing in this box?"

Diane was entranced in the details of the will and failed to notice her husband's reaction as he read the paperwork in front of him until he exclaimed, "Diane, have a look at this."

Diane leaned over the table, her gaze drawn to the faded writing on the paper, handwritten notes in a style she knew well. It was written by her husband and dated over thirty years prior. Diane could feel her heart race as she read the words, their meaning becoming clear.

"Albert, do you realize what this is?"

"Notes from a divorce case. I must have interviewed Mrs. Tamarland regarding the matter of a divorce. Yet she was never divorced," he said as he moved quickly to his feet and exited the conference room before Diane could ask him a single question.

Ten minutes later, he set a box of files on the conference table. Flipping through the box, he removed a sizable file stuffed with paperwork. As he rifled through the pages, Diane tried to restrain herself. She was overwhelmed with curiosity until he handed a photocopy of the notes that he found in the enormous file, "There it is, that would explain it."

Diane could no longer wait, "Explain what?"

"Why I completely forgot about this case, it was so long ago and Mrs. Tamarland was a witness and not a defendant or a plaintiff."

"What case is that?"

"The Beacourt case. I represented Doctor Grant Beacourt."

Diane remembered a kind, older man that served the residents of Apple Mews for many years. "I did not know he was divorced. I thought he was only married one time."

"To be entirely honest I had forgotten about it. He was married briefly to a woman who sued him for divorce citing infidelity. Mrs. Tamarland was subpoenaed, she was one of three women with whom he had allegedly conducted relations. The evidence was circumstantial and I defended the doctor and won the case. He was granted a divorce and proven innocent of all charges."

"Who were the other two women cited in the case?"

Albert read over the notes of the case and his answer was one of surprise. "Joan Rigdon and Eileen Campbell."

"That was over thirty years ago, I wonder where they are now," Diane said as she reached for her mobile phone.

She reached Inspector Crothers' voicemail and left a message as she made notes regarding the case. Mrs. Tamarland was a witness in a case that was over thirty years old and may not have any bearing on her murder, but it was possible and as frustrated as Diane and Inspector Crothers were regarding these murders, any possible lead was well worth researching.

Diane and Albert continued searching through the files but found nothing else in Mrs. Tamarland's history to rival the divorce case. They discovered that the other two women and the former Mrs. Beacourt were not clients of Albert's firm. As Diane and Albert tidied up the files and cleaned up the conference room, Inspector Crothers returned her call.

"Inspector, please tell me that your day was productive."

"No, I am afraid to say that we are back to square one, Mrs. Hedley was an interesting lead but she proved to be a dead end. Sergeant Webster thinks he may have found something at Mrs. Tamarland's residence, a piece of mail we missed on a previous search, but that is where we stand at the moment."

Diane was disappointed to hear that the Inspector was no closer to solving the case. She could hear the sound of disappointment in his voice, the days of exhaustion taking their toll. "I may have something for you, are you in a position to write down a few names?"

"Names?" he said. "Plural?"

"I am not going to lie to you, this may be nothing, but it's the best we've got right now. Do you remember Doctor Beacourt?"

"I do, but he died last autumn, how is he connected to this business?"

Mrs. Tamarland was named in his divorce case, she and two other women."

"Named how?"

"She was accused of infidelity with the doctor. She appeared in court as did two other women who would be around my age if they were still alive."

"That seems slim, but I will take it considering I have nothing to go on."

"Check out Miss Joan Rigdon and Eileen Campbell, they may have married since this case went to court."

"Ask him about Mrs. Beatrice Beacourt," added Albert.

"Be sure to check into the other woman, the ex-wife of the doctor, she would be in the same age group as well."

"I will research these people and get back to you. They would be the same age as our victims, there may be something to that. Joan may be a common name, but that was the first name of Mrs. Cranston Buxby."

Diane wished him good luck as she powered off the phone. Looking at Albert, she picked up a box of files and followed him out of the conference room.

Chapter 13

The drive home was unusually quiet as Albert and Diane were both lost in their own thoughts. Diane wanted to be hopeful that she had information that the Inspector could use in the investigation but the other three names in the case were not familiar. It seemed promising and also a dead end, just like everything else in this case.

Albert's silence was caused by another reason, a reason he soon revealed. "Diane, I pray that the murderer is found soon, but I have to confess, I hope this divorce case is not the connection you have been looking for."

"Albert, whatever do you mean? I hope it is."

"Diane, if it is then I am at fault, I am equally as guilty as the murderer of killing Mrs. Buxby."

To say that Diane was in shock was an understatement. "You guilty? Albert, how can that be?"

"Inspector Crothers asked me if I remembered anything about Mrs. Tamarland, anything of a legal nature and I said no. If I had only remembered this case, would that have made any difference?"

"You can't blame yourself, how were you supposed to remember every single client, every single meeting or case? What's important is that you may have helped solve this case if any of this information proves to be useful."

Albert nodded his head slowly. "If you think so."

"I do," Diane replied as the mobile phone rang in her hand. It was Inspector Crothers.

"Diane, you and your husband are to be commended, Miss Joan Rigdon married and became Mrs. Cranston Buxby."

"And Miss Campbell?"

"Never married but lived in Durry before her untimely death early this year of anaphylactic shock, a reaction which, according to the notes from the coroner, was brought on by something she consumed at tea. It was never investigated as a murder by the police in that county because it was ruled accidental."

"All three are dead after tea?"

"Yes, and you may find this interesting. Mrs. Beatrice Beaufort, the ex-wife, goes by a different name now."

"Anyone we know?" asked Diane as she held her breath.

"Her full name is Beatrice Edie Morgan, she changed back to her maiden name after the divorce, she lives in Shrewsbury, but she has recently attended church in her old parish, right here in Apple Mews."

"Edie Morgan? I was introduced to her at church. It's funny that I don't remember her all those years ago, I should, she used to live here."

"She is nearly fifteen years older than you and lived in Manchester for the better part of the last three decades, I would be surprised should you have known her. I am astonished she is still alive. She must be spry because she still has a car registered to her name and a driver's license."

"Inspector, with your permission I would like to pay a visit to her, she may be in grave danger."

"It may not be safe, she could be the next victim. I will post an officer to guard her residence until I can locate a suspect."

"I promise I will be careful, there will be an officer nearby. Just text her address to me and I will see how she is doing."

Inspector Crothers reluctantly agreed as Diane powered off the phone. She knew that Albert was taking this to heart and she patted his arm as he drove. "Albert, the first woman died before Mrs. Tamarland, you can't blame yourself."

"I know, but I still feel to blame."

"Don't, you may be the reason that Apple Mews can sleep safer tonight, you may have solved this mystery."

Chapter 14

Diane slept fitfully that night as she waited for morning. Albert fell asleep after a nightcap, his guilt temporarily assuaged by single malt. In the morning Diane was awake with the sunrise. She did not have an appetite, although she tried to show her appreciation for Deirdre's efforts by eating as much of the whole wheat oats and fresh fruit as she could. Dressing for a morning's errands, she kissed Albert goodbye. The frustration of the unsolved case was gone, and in its place there was anxiety. She hoped to arrive in Shrewsbury in time to save Edie Morgan.

Checking the address as she crossed the border of the city limits, Diane carefully drove through traffic until she reached a modern apartment building. Parking the car, she was amazed that at first glance, the building appeared like any other contemporary design - sleek with cheerful landscaping to mask the steel girders and concrete. This was not the kind of place she expected to find a woman older than herself.

A concierge greeted her at the entrance as she walked to the elevators. The address that the Inspector texted to her was correct. As she waited patiently for the elevator doors to close, she read a sign prominently displayed above the lighted buttons for the floors. This was an assisted living retirement community, its sleek lines blending in with the modern architecture of the expanding city limits of Shrewsbury.

Stepping from the elevator, she wondered how the officer posted outside would ever be able to monitor any visitors that Miss Morgan may have or keep her safe. It was a question she would pose later, she thought as she walked down the corridor.

Diane approached a brightly painted door that was decorated with a floral wreath. Raising her hand, she wrapped her fingers around the knocker. Inside the residence, a dog barked. From the sound of its voice, Diane knew it to be a small one, a Chihuahua or a Pomeranian or something else equally tiny.

Knocking on the door only caused the little dog to bark excitedly as Diane wondered if anyone was at home. A voice on the other side of the door called out, "Who is it?"

"Diane Dimbleby from church."

"Do I know you?"

Diane wondered if she was standing in front of the right door, "Miss Morgan?"

"Yes?"

"It's Diane, I met you at church."

"Diane, that's right, married to Albert," the woman said from the other side as she unlocked the door.

The door opened and out bounced a terrier, a gray streak of lightning that barked at her from the hallway.

"Oscar, get back in here this minute."

The dog glared at Diane as she was invited into the modern apartment. An open floor plan connected the kitchen to the living room, a television blared from the corner, and a large picture window displayed a view of the city.

"Let me make you some tea my dear, sit down. I apologize for not remembering you; at my age, I don't hear so good."

"Quite alright, my husband and I met you at church," Diane said as she sat down on the couch.

"Let me turn off that television, so we can have a proper chat."

The old woman shuffled in front of Diane. Her posture was slumped and her hair was gray, cut short, her eyes were bright and she moved surprisingly quickly for her age, or so Diane thought.

"I don't mean to bother you Miss Morgan, but the reason I have come to see you is to make sure you are safe."

"Safe?" asked the older women as she put the kettle on.

Oscar the terrier jumped on the couch and sat beside Diane. He stared at her, his head turned to the side.

"Does he bite?'

"No, once he gets to know you he is harmless. He is a sweet boy and I am worried about him."

The kettle whistled as Oscar and Diane stared at each other. Diane reached out to pet the little dog as Miss Morgan set down a tea tray on the coffee table.

"I don't normally receive visitors, I hope you like chocolate biscuits."

"Yes ma'am."

"You said you wanted to be sure that I am safe?"

Diane was not sure how to word what she needed to say, so simply decided to be honest, "I don't want to alarm you, but there is someone in Shropshire that has murdered two women, and possibly a third. They seem to be connected and I am afraid that you may be targeted."

"It is very thoughtful of you to drive all the way here from Apple Mews, but I assure you I am safe. Tea?" Miss Morgan asked as she poured the steaming hot liquid into a cup.

"You may be, you do have a concierge that could provide security," Diane replied.

"Oh no dearie, that is not the reason I am safe. I am safe simply because I have no one left on my list."

Diane reached for the cup of tea and wondered if she had heard the older woman correctly. "Your list?"

"Yes, you see I am dying and I had a list that I wanted to complete before I died. I have finished it, so I am ready to go now. I want to be buried in the churchyard in Apple Mews near my husband but that is all I have left to do, that and find a good home for Oscar."

Diane slowly put the tea and its saucer down on the table as she looked at the old woman. She felt confused.

"Oh dear, Oscar," the woman said as she addressed the terrier, "we have upset our guest. Let me help you, I think the young people call it a bucket list, does that help?"

"Miss Morgan, the people on your list, they would not happen to be the murder victims, would they?"

"Yes, indeed they are!" said the woman as she reached for a sweet. "Do try one of these biscuits, they are the best."

Diane felt her world spinning out of control; this kindly older woman was confessing to multiple murders and smiling about it. "Miss Morgan, maybe you are confused?"

"Not at all, my mind is sharp as a tack, these women had affairs with my husband and caused our break-up. I waited until after he was dead so I wouldn't upset him and then I took care of each one."

"Took care of, you mean murdered?"

"Yes, the first one was easy. I remember from my days working at my husband's office that she was allergic to almonds and nuts. I made her death look like an accident, a tin of tea biscuits did the trick. I have been planning this for a long time, can you tell? The second one was lucky for me, no neighbors or witnesses, a quick shot with my little gun and she was gone. The last one met me for tea; poisoning her was easy as pie when she excused herself to the powder room."

Diane thought of the gun. She was in the presence of a murderer. She felt a cold chill climb up her spine as she stared at the cup of tea in front of her. Miss Morgan may try to poison her or shoot her; either way, she could be dead soon.

"Miss Morgan, I don't know what to say, perhaps I better go."

"Not yet, stay for just a little while longer, you are quite safe. You didn't run around with my husband so I have no reason not to like you, none in the least."

"You do know you had gotten away with this crime until you confessed. I thought you were a victim."

"I must admit I am disappointed in the Inspector. I hid my tracks just long enough to get away with all three murders. I was rather hoping he would be around to arrest me."

Diane was flabbergasted as she stared at the woman seated across from her. "You want to be caught? You said you were dying, are you sure you want to spend the remaining days of your life in jail?"

"It will be worth it. I will finally be able to tell the world about these lying adulterous women and what they did to deserve being murdered. I know you aren't the police, but a confession to you is as good as anyone. Oscar likes you, and I can tell you like him. Promise me you will take care of my little boy and I will let you walk out of here," the woman said as she slid the small gun from her pocket.

She had never been held at gunpoint before, or met a woman that confessed to a triple murder. "There is a lot about this that bothers me, but I have one question. How did you get these women to agree to see you?"

"That was easy too. Turns out that if you write a nice card or letter or make a phone call, you can convince a person you want to reconcile with them before you die. That's not all, you can even talk them into meeting for tea, who can turn down tea?"

"You preyed upon their kindness, doesn't that bother you?"

"Not in the least. Now, about Oscar?"

"Oscar will be fine, I promise you, he is innocent and my husband and I could be persuaded into giving him a good home. What about you? What are you going to do? I can't forget this conversation happened."

"I don't want you to forget. Once you agree to take Oscar with you, you and I will take a little drive, you can take me to the police station. I can turn myself in. I was planning to confess this weekend but with you here,

I will let you drive. I hate driving these modern cars. I don't care for power steering."

"How do I know you won't kill me?" Diane asked.

"Just be a good girl, it's not your fault you are married to that man that represented my husband in court, I forgive you."

"Albert, he isn't on your list, is he?"

"No, although he should have been. I didn't want to get greedy, I only killed those women that were personally responsible for ruining my marriage. I am not a bad person, it would have been wrong to kill anyone else."

"Miss Morgan, how about we don't drive anywhere. I can call a good friend of mine, the Inspector, and I am sure he will drop everything he is doing and come right over."

The older woman put the gun down and smiled, "That is a better idea, it will give you and Oscar an opportunity to become friends."

"Yes ma'am, it will," Diane said as she reached into her purse and removed her phone.

"Invite that nice Inspector around for tea, I don't know a man or woman alive that doesn't love a good spot of tea."

Diane put the phone to her ear and waited for Inspector Crothers to answer. As she looked at the tea in her cup, she decided that she would not invite him or anyone else to tea ever again. She was certain that the Inspector, like herself, would see tea differently for the rest of their lives. As his familiar voice answered the phone, she considered switching to coffee starting first thing the following morning.

Get Your Free Copy of
"Murder at the Inn"

Don't forget to grab your free copy of Penelope Sotheby's first novella *Murder At The Inn* while you still can.

Go to http://fantasticfiction.info/murder-at-the-inn/ to find out more.

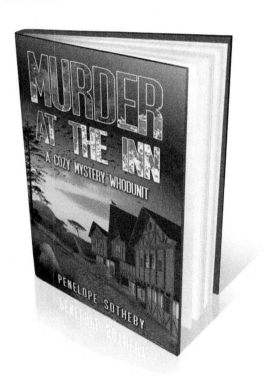

Other Books by This Author

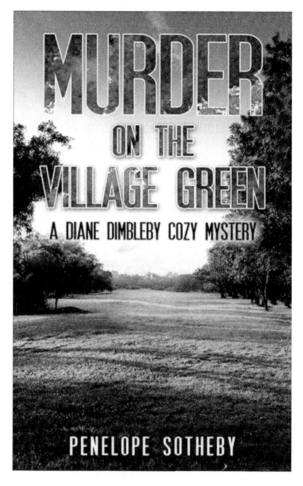

Murder on the Village Green

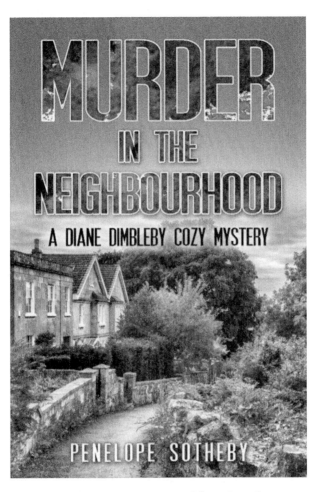

Murder in the Neighbourhood

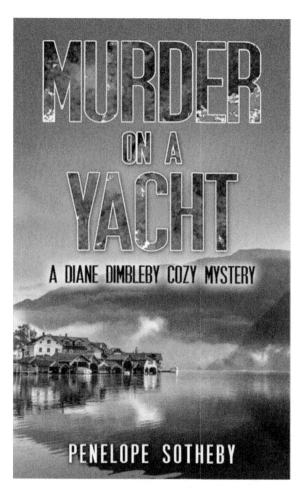

Murder on a Yacht

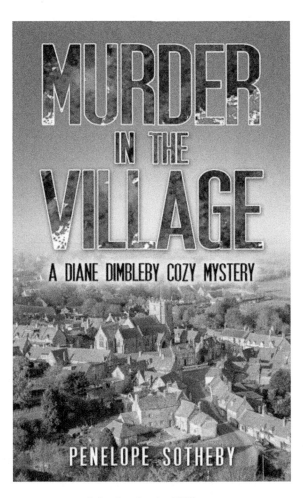

Murder in the Village

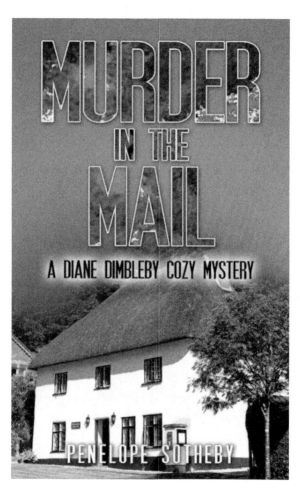

Murder in the Mail

Murder in the Development

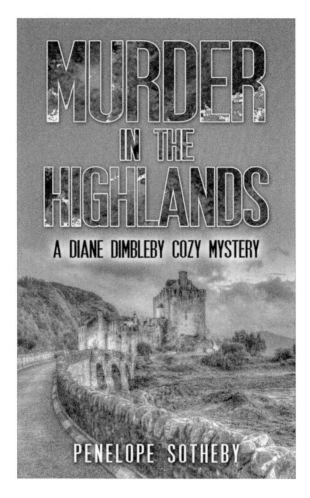

Murder in the Highlands

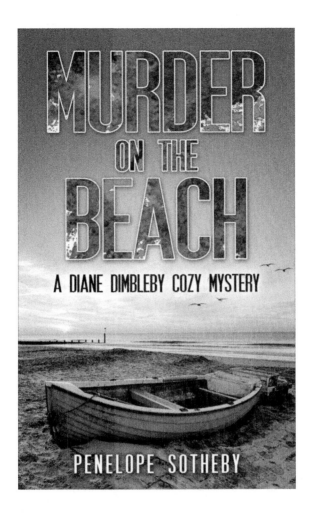

Murder on the Beach

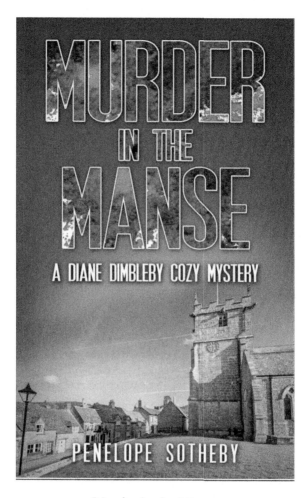

Murder in the Manse

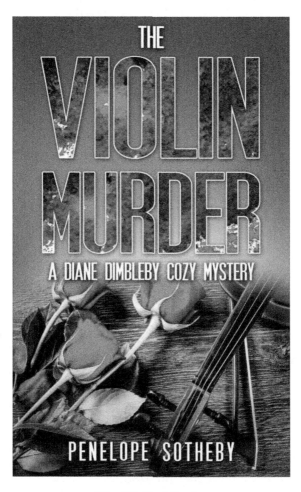

The Violin Murder

About The Author

For many, the thought of childhood conjures images of hopscotch games in quiet neighbourhoods, and sticky visits to the local sweet shop. For Penelope Sotheby, childhood meant bathing in Bermuda, jiving in Jamaica and exploring a string of strange and exotic British territories with her nomadic family. New friends would come and go, but her constant companion was an old, battered collection of Agatha Christie novels that filled her hours with intrigue and wonder.

Penelope would go on to read every single one of Christie's sixty-six novels—multiple times—and so was born a love of suspense than can be found in Sotheby's own works today.

In 2011 the author debuted with *"Murder at the Inn"*, a whodunit novella set on Graham Island off the West Coast of Canada. After receiving positive acclaim, Sotheby went on to write the series *"Murder in Paradise"*; five novels following the antics of a wedding planner navigating nuptials (and crime scenes) in the tropical locations of Sotheby's formative years.

An avid gardener, proud mother, and passionate host of Murder Mystery weekends, Sotheby can often be found at her large oak table, gleefully plotting the demise of her friends, tricky twists and grand reveals.

Fantastic Fiction

Fantastic Fiction publishes short reads that feature stories in a series of five or more books. Specializing in genres such as Mystery, Thriller, Fantasy and Sci Fi, our novels are exciting and put our readers at the edge of their seats.

Each of our novellas range around 20,000 words each and are perfect for short afternoon reads. Most of the stories published through Fantastic Fiction are escapist fiction and allow readers to indulge in their imagination through well written, powerful and descriptive stories.

Why Fiction?

At Fantastic Fiction, we believe that life doesn't get much better than kicking back and reading a gripping piece of fiction. We are passionate about supporting independent writers and believe that the world should have access to this incredible works of fiction. Through our store we provide a diverse range of fiction that is sure to satisfy.

www.fantasticfiction.info

Printed in Great Britain
by Amazon

32049309R00078